THE ORATORIO THAT WAS TIME

THE ORATORIO THAT WAS TIME

FOURTEEN POEMS AND THREE STORIES

Robert Morgan

FOREWORD BY HELENA MARÍA VIRAMONTES

AUDUBON TERRACE PRESS
New York

Some poems in this book were published in slightly different versions in *Appalachian Journal, Appalachian Places, Cloudbank, Here, Pisgah Review,* and *Terrain.org.*

Poems and stories copyright © 2022 Robert Morgan
Foreword copyright © 2022 Helena María Viramontes
All rights reserved

Editors: Bhisham Bherwani and Nicholas Birns
Cover painting: Shirley Brutko, *Cicero Ward Mountain,* watercolor, 2012
Design: Rita Lascaro

ISBN: 978-0-9972547-2-3
Library of Congress Control Number: 2022945393

Published in New York, NY by Audubon Terrace Press
Manufactured in the United States of America

First Edition

Contents

Foreword vii

POEMS

I

1948	5
Because He'd Lived So Long a Bachelor	6
Wise Virgin	7
My Father's Bible	8
Words Are Threats	9
Adoration	10
Rolling Rocks	11
Marbles	12
Harmonica	13
Purple Rags	14
Closure	15
Red Letters	16
Acrid	17

II

The Oratorio That Was Time	21

STORIES

Survey	29
War No More	45
Jack	61

Foreword

At the heart of Robert Morgan's latest and much anticipated collection, *The Oratorio That Was Time*, is reverence: in time, geographical setting, humming memories, and the shadows of consecrated narratives known as history. Sensually measured by objects of the past, by the regal sense of their shattering, his poems and stories both unspool between the marvelous and mundane, between the fantastic and fact, between memory and cross-generational history. In Morgan's poems, commonplace objects like marbles and harmonicas are raised to sacredness by the touch and tune of willful observations; we experience the glow of the stove where his father, "with hair both wet and groomed," sat to read his Bible; the "apocalyptic radiance" of icy stalactites and stalagmites becoming "chandeliers"; purple factory cloths "for wiping hands" becoming "hues of kings and amethyst"; a church bell, "like a bucket," emptying "out its startle."

Morgan's three stories are vivid reminders that our physical and moral worlds exist in tensions of past history and influence our present. In the story "Survey," an eighteenth-century surveyor is hired to document the new geography of Carolina. Within his absolute appreciation of natural beauty of the New World (also knowing its dangers) the surveyor begins to question his trespass in Native American lands. Nonetheless, having finally reached the zenith of his journey, his joy is overshadowed by a darkened vision both surreal and inevitable. "Jack" is told with a simplicity that veils the complicity of an old man's loss of memory and love. In "War No More," truly one of the finest stories about war, Morgan's skill as a historian comes into play as we follow a deserter in the Civil War, a story of survival and love with an ending that warrants astonishment.

Morgan is without comparison in writing about intergenerational history and geography, where we can uproot ourselves but never quite shake off the soil. He remains a mediator of daily experiences and these generous and intimate images and stories can only arise from a writer given over to the qualities of grace and gratitude, one who holds an equitable vision of the world. That and a profound belief in love as well.

Helena María Viramontes

POEMS

I

1948

The flowers on Grandma's grave were heaped
so thick and close they seemed more like
a compost pile than decorations.
I knew they came from shops in town
and not from any local soil.
The roses, gladioli, ferns,
and many colors of carnations,
looked like a clutter of redundancy
compared to the geraniums
and dahlias spaced so carefully
around her yard, illuminating
the bare, swept ground. I watched them hide
with blossoms brought from far away
the place they sank her body in
the red-hot clay, far from the heaven
they said was her destination.

BECAUSE HE'D LIVED SO LONG A BACHELOR

Because he'd lived so long a bachelor
before marrying, before begetting us,
my father always washed his own work clothes
in tubs of suds out on the porch,
and sewed the patches on his overalls
and faded shirts himself, the needle dwarfed
by his enormous work-swelled hands
almost as large as baseball gloves,
his fingers bent by age and weathering.
My mother never was allowed to clean
or mend the soiled and worn apparel.
There was something paradoxical about
his grasp, more used to axe and crosscut saw,
or hoe and shovel handle, drawing the all
but invisible thread in and out of denim
or khaki while sitting on the back porch steps
to get the brightest sun, and resting from
his daylong toil. Because he had remained
a bachelor so long, my father didn't
shave till after supper, or comb his hair,
a habit from his courting days he liked to joke.
With unexpected delicacy he creamed
his cheeks and chin and upper lip
and then caressed the foam off with
a flashing razor, wiped the froth from tender skin.
And only then, with hair both wet and groomed,
would he sit down beside the stove
to turn the pages of his Bible with
such care and concentration that it seemed
he read oblivious to all around
and unconnected to this time and place,
in a dispensation unfamiliar
because he'd lived so long a bachelor.

WISE VIRGIN

Aunt Wessie never could be tied
completely down in her last days
in the expensive nursing home.
The nurses were afraid she'd fall
again if left to wander in
the halls. They strapped her to the bed
with belts and cords. But in the dark
she always freed herself somehow.
Her mind, confused by day, would come
alert in darkness with the cunning
of an elderly Houdini to
get loose, explore the secret nooks,
remote extensions of the large
facility, and look into
the most forbidden zones and rooms,
the offices and pharmacy,
the farthest wing of hospice care.
They often found her in the chapel,
imagining she was in a church,
the one attended years before.
They never figured how she worked
the shackles free, arthritic hands
and stroke-numbed legs, performing tasks
the young would find a challenge. In
the darkness with no help she did
the tricks of a contortionist.
One night she dumped a pitcher of
cold water on her roommate's face,
as though to douse a threatening fire,
committed to her vigil to
the very end, determined to
be on her feet and ready as
a waiting bride, oil in her lamp,
when death came asking for her hand.

MY FATHER'S BIBLE

It lies there on a shelf among
old books and magazines and whatnots,
unmoved for twenty years or more.
The leather binding's worn along
the spine from where he held it day
by day in his large work-rough hands.
The pages too are stained and foxed
by oil or sweat and age from his
long poring over passages
again, again. Insomniac,
he liked to start a fire and read,
sip coffee hours before first light,
before the rest of us appeared.
The leaves, as thin as paper on
a cigarette, will open to
a photograph of Mama, me,
and Sister, posed before the gate
when I was maybe two or three,
the sepia faded almost white,
as though the ink had been bleached out
by strength of his long scrutiny.

WORDS ARE THREATS

When he was born his tongue was stitched
down by a thread of flesh so tight
he couldn't cry, and strained to make
a sound. A few days later doctors
snipped the muscle free, to rage
and protest, gurgle happiness,
and later speak, to utter from
the little monster melodies
as well as narratives and lies.
Yet still at times the site of taste
will freeze as if surprised
by unforeseen paralysis,
refuse delivery of intent
in fear of language itself
and threat of no command of tongue,
to wallow in the dark and mud
of swamps and quicksand trap,
where words become an enemy,
then wonderful when rule returns.

ADORATION

When I was three an awful ice
storm hit on Christmas Day. As I
looked out the kitchen door the world
appeared encased in glass.
The hemlocks dragged their wings so low
they seemed embarrassed and ashamed
to be so bowed. As trees broke in
the woods they sounded loud as guns
or fireworks for the holiday.
Porch steps glazed and rounded off
were dangerous. The clothesline and
the fence were magnified by ice
as if seen through binoculars.
Though shivering, it all appeared
a little subterranean
to me, stalactites and stalagmites,
where things had dripped and set.
But suddenly the sun shot through
apocalyptic radiance,
and wind began to shake the trees.
A million chandeliers crashed hard,
as if all the stars of heaven
and all the glitter of the season
were shattering in adoration.

ROLLING ROCKS

To set a flat rock up and give
a shove and see its cornered shape
become a wheel and blur with speed,
jump over logs and other rocks,
remaining vertical and fast,
exhilarated us. Round rocks
were fun but obvious. It was
the awkward ones that took some skill
to make them start and stay upright.
Was it a sense of power to watch
the heavy ones accelerate
and even fly? Or was it more
a satisfaction to move chunks
and pieces of the summit to
the lower slopes? It seemed an act
of conjuring to yield the rocks
to gravity and let them soar,
like launching kites or giving stones
an independent life to spin
long after we let go of them,
to lower elevations, out
of sight, though we could hear their noise
in leaves, like we had given spark
to the inanimate, at least
for the descent, spun wild and free
as we ourselves would like to be.

MARBLES

You scratch a circle on the ground
to be a field of battle, then
place all the pot of marbles at
the center in a pod. And next you
aim a favorite shooter with
your thumb, for this is war. You pick
them off like Sergeant York, who took
a company of German soldiers,
and drive as many as you can
out of the ring, collecting all
that roll beyond the boundary
as booty. Best of shooters is
a buckshot-sized ball bearing to
flick off with a spin to burst
the cluster, stick in place to fire
again to empty out the nest
before opponents get their chance.
You bend on knees as though in prayer
to blast the cat eyes, reds, and blues,
to claim before the teacher's bell.
They rattle in your pocket with
the sound of victory as you walk,
your knuckles raw from grinding dirt,
through fragrant April air.

HARMONICA

Sent back from wartime Britain with
my Uncle Robert's last effects,
the instrument was gold with red
inside where notes were made. I put
it to my lips and blew a chord
at once exotic and familiar,
the holes aligned like seeds on cobs.
He must have bought it over there
to ease himself in hours and nights
between the raids above the flak
and oxygen of Germany,
the mouth organ enhancing vowels
of voice, and left behind for his
return. I cupped the music in my hands
as though to shield it from all sight
and threatening wind, a flame of memory
in search of Cold War harmony.

PURPLE RAGS

In factories and shops where grease
was integral to every task
and part, there used to be these rags
of fabric, coarse yet smooth and tough,
a certain shade of purple cloth
for wiping hands and rubbing down
machines and tools. That lavender
was chosen for these handkerchiefs
might seem at first a paradox,
the royal color to be smeared
with darkest stains day after day,
absorbing filth and solvents' reek
from hands of foulest work, from steel
with grit and soot and oil stuck to it.
Yet purple was appropriate
to the nobility of work,
essential to the cleaning and repair
in pits, the dignity of sweat
and knuckles cracked and pores all black,
to keep the world's clock chiming with
the poetry of time itself,
the calluses of palms caressed
with hues of kings and amethyst.

CLOSURES

So many places where I used
to walk are now closed off, the trail
around the Cicero that came
out on the summit like a path
into an upper realm, the way
along the river bank beneath
the birches, sycamores, and vines,
the route across the pasture to
the pines and whispering branch, then by
the old molasses furnace built
by Grandpa Morgan years before
my birth, all fenced and posted by
the owners of new houses who
will tolerate no trespassing
on property once open, clear.
So all that's left is just the road
now paved and widened, though the dogs
behind the fences growl and bark
at anyone on foot and make
a quiet stroll impossible,
and privacy unfeasible.
While those inside the houses stroll
and troll the internet and strive
in games on screens for hour on hour
are unaware that clouds parade
majestically above, that paths
once led to higher elevations.

RED LETTERS

For reasons now no longer clear
it seemed a most important thing
to set his name in the bare dirt
before the gate of the henhouse.
The letters must be boldly cut
and hollowed to a certain depth,
then filled with brightest, reddest clay,
so every letter shines out loud
inlaid in ordinary soil.
It seemed essential to him that
the name embedded in the yard
appear as perfect as the script
on some official monument,
writ large for all posterity
in contrast to surrounding ground.
It was imperative that he
inset in brilliant color those
brave letters of identity
he'd only learned a year before.
He toiled throughout the afternoon
to gouge the tracks precise, then get
the blood-dark clay from the road bank
and fill the characters with care
to finest definition, then
stood back to admire his art
before the chickens must be fed.
Next day he found the hens had scratched
his best artistic efforts blank,
and rain had washed the red from his
first venture at celebrity.

ACRID

The urine smell of boxwoods in
old yards suggests the vigor and
the reek of those who left their sweat
and water in this soil for years.
As dogs will mark their boundaries
and priests their services, these little trees
proclaim by scent dominion for
the dead, the vital salty stink
still lingering and organic,
alive as breath or tears or wind,
and redolent of work and drink,
of standing on the porch at night
to ease a bladder pressing tight,
or emptying a chamber pot.
We recognize the ancient smart
of evergreens both small and airy
as scent of our acridity.

II

THE ORATORIO THAT WAS TIME

From his earliest memory he had been
able to make music in his head.
Whatever he was doing, wherever he was running,
playing with a toy airplane, hammering wood,
awake in bed at night, he heard music
to accompany what he did or thought.
The music was there in mind to match
the other senses, a correlative
to the world around him, but also
a kind of grammar for his feelings, for the story
of his life, like music on the radio
to direct, heighten, and define attention.

The music in his head was made of fragments
of things heard, of hymns and Christmas carols,
gospel music, country, western, also choral
and organ pieces savored on the radio.
Sometimes the set on Saturday
would offer concerts of the Philharmonic.
The Philadelphia Orchestra was sponsored by
Longines once a week, and he
imagined fine watches with the finest music,
though he'd never actually seen a Longines watch.

A passage that would haunt him, recalled
and played again, again in thought,
embellishing the tune with variations,
was a theme he learned much later came
from Bach's fifth Brandenburg. He must have heard
it on the radio. The melody came back
to him at any time, to lift his spirits,
confidence, to make the world seem firm
and meaningful. He relished the word *orchestra*,
unsure exactly what it meant. He loved

also the groan and rumble and deep
bowel music of the organ with its high, bright trills
and twitter in the upper registers.
And knowing nothing of the violin and cello,
he memorized a theme he later learned
was from Four Seasons of Vivaldi.

Something noticed in the church was that
while individual voices might not please
it made a difference when more voices
joined together. He could not explain the effect,
but knew it true. All singing at once
would surprisingly enrich the air,
invigorating time. When people sang
on the riverbank at baptizing there was
a conjure to it, the sound of the river,
the trees, and light on water, the candidates
in white, and voices reaching over water.

And the church bell echoing across the valley
on Sunday morning was a special kind of tune,
one note resounding, splashing out, and washed to
the mountain and back, and up the river valley.
He'd seen Uncle Allen ring the bell, pulling down
the rope like the starting cord of a motor.
And the bell in the steeple, like a bucket,
emptied out its startle to the farthest coves and hollows.
Once the bell was rung on workday evenings
for a revival, and another uncle,
not known to be musical, would stop his work
to listen to the summoning note.

The world outside could brim with music.
Some mornings a dove called through the fog or mist

a sad but dignifying note. A mockingbird
debuted from the Wolf River apple tree and quoted
both other birds and noises, repeating and varying
its song, weaving permutations and echoes.
The cardinal had a wet, fresh note, the joree
a quick and teasing call. A hawk whistled high,
and circled, spotting mice or chickens in a field.
Crows quarreled from oaks on Squirrel Hill.
And the whistle from the cotton mill would sound
like no other note at noon and quitting time.
Sometimes a fox barked on the mountainside.

At the house by the river he'd heard
the whippoorwills keep him awake.
And there were owls in the trees above the house,
screech owls, hoot owls, and what was called
a laughing owl that sounded like hysteria
in the dark. Nothing could be better than
the call of quail, the bobwhite, from brush around
the edges of the orchard, the call so gentle, calm,
it made the day seem peaceful. And the dove
made you feel so lonely you would shudder.

On a closer, quieter scale, there was no music
more soothing than a cricket in late summer grass
beside the trail, in weeds behind the house.
The cricket struck black tones from its flint,
a plainsong of the summer's end, of yellow leaves
and cooler evenings. Best of all, a larger cricket,
the meadow mole, made notes so deep and slow,
a melancholy tolling of delicious sadness
in weeds soon to be burned by frost.

There was a music of the inanimate too,
in the drum and hum of rain on the barn's tin roof,
on gray autumn afternoons. Wind sang in eaves
of the barn and through the corncrib cracks.
The roaring in the hemlocks in a storm
was a raving, feral music, and sighing
in the white pines on a quiet day was another strain.
Wherever he would turn there would be song:
the drip of water in a pool below
the outdoor faucet, the murmur of a branch.

By the river he heard whispers and muttering current
far from the shoals. Water leapt in a tongue
from the pipe in the springhouse, reciting something
much like poetry. Jarflies played dry jazz
in the late summer oaks, and katydids would chant
throughout the night their love-call fanfares.

The loudest music was the thunder crashing
like barrels overhead. The rhythms of thunder
were irregular, echoing lightning's signal.
He saw the burning fuse of lightning fall
and heard a snap in air as though a switch were thrown,
and then the blast and crackling like the growls
of cosmic bullies. Every peal was different
in intensity, in phrasing and duration, and
each clapper came from a farther part of sky.
A blast could be so loud and close he felt
the shock waves ripple through his flesh.

And late at night he listened to the music
of the house, the groan of walls as the old
structure settled, the ring of cooling tin on roof,
the knock on walls, the creak of attic steps,

a rattle in the loft. And there was music
in the stillness itself, of air almost
at rest, the close maraca thresh of silence.
For moments then the air would seem to sleep,
with balance, poise, go on and on until
a nail would growl along a sill, a mouse
scratch in the wall, a dog howl farther up the valley.
And then he floated in the song of sleep,
the long oratorio that was time.

STORIES

Survey

JUNE 6, 1711. This notebook is my best weapon of defense. I have a pistol and a musket on my packhorse, but if the natives are watching, as they likely are, they could send their poison arrows from an ambush, and I'd have no time to defend myself with either firearm or sword. But the Indians fear writing, or at least are mystified by the act of fixing words on a page. It may also be they think me a harmless fool, laboring miles day after day, making marks and drawing pictures of flowers, trees, fauna, and rivers, collecting roots, leaves, bark, and berries.

I keep my compass concealed, because I'm told the aborigines hate the instrument, and call it "land-stealer," having seen surveyors make lines on territory that will never be their hunting ground again. Hopefully, they won't know I'm a surveyor, though I'm not the kind that divides land into acres and hectors, but explores and describes. The Lord Proprietors have commissioned me once again to peregrinate and record the richness and resources of the colony, to attract new residents to this latitude of the New World, called Carolina, named for the late King Charles. So, I begin my mission into the backcountry.

It worries me that the Tuscarora have allied themselves with other clans to punish the whites who've settled and established claims to this fair wilderness. Many settlers have been killed, their habitations burned. My hope is to avoid all hostilities, display only interest in the cause of science. But as I wander into the interior, I feel natives study my every step. The forest and the shrubbery have eyes, and the air has ears. I must not let myself be daunted, but proceed as though in perfect safety, compiling catalogues and descriptions.

The pines I've passed through bleed resin that reminds me of the sperm of candles. Where a limb has broken or a woodpecker hammered, the gum drips and runs down the bark, looking sugary. Today I've followed Hunters' Trail along the river. The trail is dangerous, because the Indians may be monitoring it. But so is every furlong of the forest. I must not risk being lost, even before I reach the hill country. My business is with the interior. I've already explored the coastal regions some years back. In the swamps and thickets

I could be lost and walk in circles for days, and never reach the uplands or mountain chain.

Today, June 18, 1711, as I made camp to cook my light repast, an arrow hummed into a tree nearby, a warning from the woods to advance no further. From the rings on the shaft I suspect it to be Tuscaroran. But it could be from another tribe as well, hoping I'll blame the Tuscarora. I ignore the gesture, and write in this notebook. If the Indians would kill me, they will. And yet the white pages of this notebook attest that I come in peace.

June 21, 1711. Today I passed the fall line of the river where water dives over the lip of bedrock, marking both the end of navigation and the onset of repeating hills. Now I'll start my work in earnest. But first I must set down what occurred last night:

I secured my horse in a little meadow by the river, and slept beside my campfire, entering the palace of dreams, when screams of the mount jerked me awake. Reaching for my pistol, I took a torch from the fire and ran toward the screams. The horse kicked and squealed, with a panther fastened to his back. I fired the pistol at its head, and the shot either missed or had no effect. The horse shrieked with pain and terror, as the big cat bit into its withers.

Forgetting the danger, I rushed toward the demon feline and thrust the torch into its evil face. The cat loosened its claws from the horse and jumped aside to disappear into the night. I tried to calm the steed; it bled where the claws had sunk in, and where the dagger teeth had gnashed. I was much too scared to sleep again that night. There are rumors of tigers in these woods, as well as panthers. Yet I will not turn back and abort my survey. If fate be with me, I will persist. If fate be against me, I will not prosper in any case.

July 1, 1711. I've reached the hill country and seen many hardwoods, maple, several kinds of oak, hickory, chestnut. The understory dogwood is prevalent, as are redbud, also the gum tree, tulip poplar, walnut. Clear springs issue from the hillsides; Virginia deer are plentiful. I've kept silent and shot no game, relying on biscuit and porridge. A gunshot would attract the natives, and I have snares for rabbits and other small game. Perhaps my Quaker childhood makes me reluctant to kill. At night wolves howl, though they could be Indians imitating beasts to frighten me. I'm told the aborigines do perfect mimicry of panthers, birds, foxes. Even as I write this, I feel the eyes of the forest piercing from the shadows. I draw images of leaves I've found, and berries.

July 7, 1711. The soil here is rich as any I've known in England, a mealy loam compiled of forest decay for millennia. Soon I hope to reach the Saponi, a noble stream sweeping through the hills from the higher mountains beyond. Hunters have found the Saponi a paradise of game and furs, even though the natives threaten. Some stretches of these hills are open prairie covered with grass of several kinds, and wild peavines. Large black and yellow bees, much bigger than honeybees, fill the air. Also a special hornet.

Today I found the path barely discernible in weeds and forest leaves, a native trace. Sometimes there are pictures scratched on rocks or trees to mark the way, unreadable to me, maybe hostile, maybe friendly. A dead polecat hung from a limb above the trail, some sort of sign, likely not welcoming. But I've continued my assignment, armed with notebook, my calculations and pictures. I won't be dissuaded.

July 14, 1711. Today I saw an eagle, lord of the air, circling high above the forest, lifted by the heated vapors. And then it dropped like a shot from a barrel, and rose with an animal in its claws, a rabbit or small rodent called a groundhog. It flapped to a lair faraway to feast on its prey, Lord of all it sees.

In the path I stumbled on a hoop with fur and feathers attached. Perhaps some warrior had dropped it there. More likely it's a sign to urge me to go back. But I will not turn back, for now. I'm entering unexplored regions. If fate permits, I'll go where only the Spanish may have searched before. I imagine I can see mountains, but know they are just banks of clouds above the hills. The wounds on my horse's back heal, slowly.

Today, July 23, 1711. I have a significant depression of spirits. First, I began to question the mission I've undertaken in this wilderness. What right do I have to invade these territories where the aborigines have hunted and lived for thousands of years? True, they have not husbanded or improved the land to any great degree, and they are pagans with no visible practice of worship or piety. Yet, I've already seen near the coast the forests felled, the game taken, the diseases the natives suffer. The Queen has given the Lord Proprietors these tracts to survey and civilize, where only darkness reigned before. Yet what natural right do we have to invade and alter?

Such thoughts have made me weary and I must push them aside, for I know the fallacy of these meditations. I understand the tribes kill each other and take land from each other in perpetual contention. They burn their enemies at the stake after much torture. And these conflicts and wars reach far back into the womb of history, to clans whose names we'll never know. And even before that, the first nations invaded the land of deer and bear, of panthers and raccoons, of fish and otter. It's the way of tribes, one subduing another, era to era. And now we bring enlightenment to these swamps and thickets, hills and woodland streams. Otherwise we'd have to think: what right do we have to breathe air or take up space in this fallen world? What countenance are we given, to speak, or see sunlight on clouds?

July 24, 1711. Only in the labor of finding my way through an endless canebrake did my spirits lift. The cane along the streams reaches twice a man's height, sometimes more. The stalks grow close together and sway and swish in the breeze. From a distance they appear alive, waving and bowing. But it's best to avoid the canes, this titanic grass, for rattlesnakes hide in their depths and gloom, and panthers. The big cats lurk and pounce. And the horse will panic in the tall brakes, brushed by whispering and breathy wands. Every stream has canes along its banks, and low spots in meadows are covered with such thickets.

As I progress into the hills, canebrakes are fewer, perhaps because the steeper ground is better drained. The hills have bolder fountains, water issuing from under acclivities, pure and cold, filling basins from pores in earth, through rocks and roots of tulip poplars. It's a special pleasure to drink from springs that look like magnifying lenses. Tiny salamanders grip sand on their floors. The ebullition causes sand to dance without ceasing.

Now I must record a wonderful phenomenon, for those who may be reading this account. As stated, I love these fountains, except for those in deep shade where mosquitoes gather, whining like bullets or distant bugles. The creatures give needles to the air, and any exposed skin will be pierced. And besides the mosquitoes, there are even smaller insects that draw blood. Only smoke will drive away the pests. I don't linger by a spring in shade.

I was about to describe a mystery, but think I've puzzled out the conundrum. Yesterday I came to a fountain in a more open place, surrounded by filbert bushes. It was a fine spring, rippling in its pool, and overflowing through a channel between rocks. I drank from its sweet humor that tasted like something that had passed through sapphires deep in ground. Then as I was about to fill my bottle, the surge stopped. At first, I wasn't sure what I saw, and then the outflow began to empty the basin. The source in the earth had been cut off. Every spring I've seen before was tireless, except in drought. How could a stream suspend before my eyes?

I stood before the shrinking pool and pondered the riddle. No law of nature I know could explain the fact witnessed. I watered the horse quickly, before the pool was emptied, then stood by, poring over the extraordinary display. Had the Indians cast a spell on this lone fountain? Then, even as I gazed, I beheld another miracle: a nostril in the sand splashed out into the basin. The stream flushed into the pool and filled to overflowing. I was too astonished to do more than gape at the ripples and deepening catchment. Had I observed witchcraft? I looked around to see if a native shaman were performing pranks. If so, he remained hidden.

I think of myself as a natural philosopher who explores and surveys the flora and fauna, the minerals, the soil, and rivers. Yet here was something no law or agent I understood could account for. Something controlled the stream and could reverse or restore the current in minutes. It could take weeks for a spring to dry up in a drought, yet here in less than five minutes the fountain had altered from spate to dearth and back to flood again. It was a puzzle too deep for me to resolve, for it violated all I know of God's ordinances. It was nature playing tricks, and I was the target of the jest.

I squandered so much time watching the ebb and flow it was late afternoon and I'd no choice but to make camp near the wonderful fountain. The phenomenon had put its spell on me. I secured the horse in a nearby meadow and took a rabbit in a snare for dinner. Even as I ate and offered a prayer for safe journey, I heard water gush forth again into the basin. Then silence ruled for a time, broken only by howls from the hills. A few minutes later, the water thrust again, periodic as a mantel clock.

As I slept, I heard water whisper or gurgle nearby and then cease. The murmur stopped, and in my dream I waited. In dreams we're sometimes half awake and know we are dreaming. In dreams we transcend logic in subtle ways, unexplained ways.

A voice spoke, as if from underground, the words "siphon" and "cistern," a voice I didn't recognize at first, then knew to be my own. And I saw a cavity in rock, inside a hill, filling with cold water in the dark. Slowly water seeped in from the hill until the cistern was full and began overflowing through an opening in the rock. But the opening acted as a siphon as the stream sank below the level of the top of the outflow, pulling water through the siphon until the cistern was bare. And then the cavity began to fill again as the spring ebbed.

It was a strange and beautiful thing, that explanation for the phenomenon, which came to me in a dream. I was so excited I slept no more last night, but sat listening to the bell of my horse. I must have floated away in sleep again, for the bell grew more distant, fading into the noises of the forest.

When I did wake, my first impulse was to observe the spring whose mystery I'd solved in my dream. The fountain was ebbing as I expected, the basin empty, except for a puddle at the bottom. Only then did I notice the stillness from the meadow. I bolted in that direction, and saw no horse. Had the steed wandered into the woods, even though tethered? Frantically, I searched the closer trees, ran to the place where I'd tethered the animal. An arrow was stuck in the ground like a message. The aborigines had taken my noble beast of burden.

I'd known the Indians had me under surveillance. Here in the wilderness, they have taken my only means of transport to convey specimens, roots, seeds, skins, musket, and necessities. Now I carry only the clothes on my back, the boots on my feet, take only what I can convey on my shoulders, in this ocean of trees and hills. Is this my punishment, for I have taken the Lord Proprietors' penny, to invade the land of the aborigines? I have taken his penny and must dance. I've my compass still, my burning glass, and telescope. Should I turn back toward the coast, toward civilization? Will the natives come for me next, for my last supplies and instruments, for my hair? Will Providence sustain me?

July 25, 1711. I've spent much of the day sorting through my baggage to decide what is essential and what may be hidden near the siphon spring. I'll conceal what I can't carry under brush to claim later. This spring is still emptying and rising, like an emblem of foul luck alternating with good fortune. I've seen the marvels of this beauteous land, but now, stripped of my means of transport, alone, must depend on my two legs to carry what is necessary. I must leave the telescope.

This morning I almost trod on the serpent called copperhead, a mottled beast that gives no warning, unlike the rattlesnake. Natives worship the rattler because it never strikes without threatening with its tail. They fear it's a particular sin to take the rattler's life. But the copperhead is sly. This one blended with the leaves and grass and struck my boot, but the leather shielded me, suffering only two dents, stained with drops of venom. Having delivered its worst, the fat viper whipped away into the peavines. I washed the boot and thanked heaven for the sturdy cowhide.

This evening as I made my fire and ate a humble repast of berries and biscuit, I contemplated returning to New Bern with the few samples I can carry. But the flames cheered me a little. A fire promotes confidence and a sense of home in the wilderness. A blaze inspires and establishes a kind of altar which the wilderness respects. As I looked into the flames I knew that I should turn east, thankful the natives have only taken my horse and left my hair and my life. But I know that at dawn I'll go forward to the west, pursuing my survey, for the wonderful, the unknown, the menacing, wait there to be found.

July 27, 1711. Yesterday I didn't write in this account. The reason was I couldn't build a fire to reveal my location. Instead I crouched in the dark all night, fearing discovery. Now I thank the Fates that I'm still alive to tell my story to the page.

Yesterday I left the ill-omened spring and found Hunters' Trail again. If the Indians already knew where I was, I'd no reason to conceal myself. But I remained alert, with the sack on my back, the musket in my hand. The weapon was loaded, but could be fired only once because the keg of powder had been left behind. I'd not gone more than a mile when I heard voices behind me. Quick as possible I stepped behind a cluster of laurels near the trail, ashamed of my cowardice. The voices grew closer, and soon a train of aborigines came in sight. Painted red and black, they carried spears and bows and arrows, tomahawks and shields. They spoke in quiet voices.

I bent low in the brush, breathing slowly. Just after the line had passed, cries, yells, screams, rose from the trail ahead. The party from one direction had met a war party from the other. The fighting must have continued for half an hour. There were grunts and shrieks; I dared not get back on the trail. Soon the first party returned, some limping and bleeding. Wounded were carried or dragged. A hundred yards behind me was a small clearing, and they stopped there to lay down the injured. I hoped they'd move on, but they stayed and made fires.

When it grew dark, the wounded sang chants as they were dying. I'd never heard such sad sounds. All night I watched as the injured sang and died. The living put leaves on their own wounds, and mud poultices. The only signs of mourning were the songs. The dead they kept out of the firelight.

In daylight the Indians were gone and had left no sign of the dead remains. Had the bodies been buried, or carried with them? Alone in the forest again, I studied my predicament and saw I must travel on Hunters' Trail no longer. I'd strike out through the woods with only my compass and the sun to guide me. And I'd not turn back, but continue the commission to the farther west.

July 28, 1711. Today the rain began. I might have found a shelter in a hollow tree, but instead I launched out. It seemed wrong to waste a day, and besides, it would be safer to travel in bad weather, when I'd have the woods to myself, as aborigines and beasts kept to their lairs. And there is an intimacy in rain, as if the senses are more acute, alert. Other things are hiding from the rain, while you are at the heart of it, vigilant in the forest. You have the advantage, for you are not hiding, but allied with the elements.

All day I traveled, my boots so wet they swished, hat dripping. Even my armpits under the coat were saturated. I knew it would be hardest to strike a fire, even though my flint and tinder were safe in their canister. But what could I use for kindling in the dripping woods? I came to a stream and rested against a maple tree. I'd now reached the higher hills, but the clouds pressed low and I could see nothing above the treetops.

As I leaned on the tree, I became aware the stream nearby rushed like a tongue and swelled to its banks. I tried to stand, and grabbed the sack, just as a wall of water lifted and hurled me away. Still gripping the sack, I spun backwards and sideways, hitting trees, flung helplessly. A laurel thicket stopped me, trapped in its limbs. I clung with my right hand to a branch, and thought I must die. The flood pulled and slapped. And then the tide slowed and dropped away, and left me tangled in the laurel limbs. I was bruised, but otherwise unhurt. It took me the rest of the day to strike a fire to dry my things. Thank heaven the pages of this notebook were not touched, wrapped in oiled leather. So I'm able to record this account. Is this tribulation a portent of things to come? Have the Fates spun my destiny to end, not in London, but in this cruel New World?

July 29, 1711. Today I whacked my way farther into the hill country. What is my purpose here? What am I learning? Without a horse I can collect few specimens. What's my life worth, penetrating these untamed lands? My father, the Quaker elder, in a village in Lincoln, warned me of my fascination with adventure, as though exploration were blasphemy. "The Lord did not intend us to encroach on the lands of the infidel unless invited," he argued. "You are exposed to grave danger." Three times I've entered the woods of Carolina, and three times through the grace of God and the tolerance of the natives have survived.

July 30, 1711. Today the great surprise was to come upon another white creature in these wilds. I avoided the trail for reasons of safety, winding through the woods at my own discretion, consulting the compass and the sun, for I know we tend to walk in circles without guidance, as one leg takes shorter steps, or our senses deceive us, or for whatever reason. I pursued my course toward higher hills, when I saw smoke ahead and smelled cooking. Halting, assuming it was a native camp, I prepared to retreat, when a figure appearing to be half-animal, half-man, stepped from behind a tree with a musket aimed at my heart. "Halt, stranger," he said, "on pain of death." He was covered with hides and furs.

I stepped back and raised my left hand and explained my mission. He demanded I swear I'd tell no one I'd seen him or the location of his camp, and I gladly complied. "I don't need no permission of no Lord Proprietor," he snorted. He invited me into his bivouac where an Indian girl of not more than sixteen stirred a pot over the fire. The girl didn't speak and the hunter didn't introduce me. Neither did he tell me his name. But he asked me to drop my pack and sit on a log. He offered a piece of steamed venison on a stick and I accepted. As I ate he explained that he preferred bear meat, but deer were easier to hunt, and he further related that he collected deer hides in summer and furs in winter. The girl was Cherokee, and because he'd married her he had hunting rights in the territory. They lived in a kind of hut made of sticks and covered with hides. He had several horns of powder and offered me one. In return I gave him six bullets from my sack. I showed him this notebook, and he said the Cherokees would respect the chronicle and my curiosity, but to beware of the Tuscarora. "They might scalp you, and they might not," he laughed.

The Indian girl avoided looking at me. Her deerskin dress had fine beadwork, as did her slippers.

The hunter told me I was right to avoid trails, but the hills ahead have many rattlesnakes. I told him I was more afraid of the Indians, because they did not give warning.

August 1, 1711. My shoulder is sore from carrying the sack. I alternate between left and right, but now both are galled. I've encountered no more nimrods, but have crossed the other hunters' trails. My greatest difficulty has been traversing the Saponi, wide as the widest street in London. For half an hour I stood on its side contemplating the best way to gain the far bank. My solution was to take off all my clothes and boots and stuff them in the sack, place the sack on my head, and swim with one arm. The rushing current swept me downstream a furlong, but I reached the far shore, then swam back for my musket. Water snakes uncoiled like corkscrews off limbs and disappeared into the river.

When I climbed out on the west bank the second time, I saw an aborigine watching me from the eastern side. He wanted me to know he'd been following, had monitored my progress. He did not gesture, only stared. I clothed myself and resumed my journey.

August 2, 1711. Today as I leapt a rill in the forest I saw a flash in the pool beneath a small cataract. I assumed it was a trout. There are many trout in these streams. The flash quivered in the current, but didn't move. I paused to look again, and what I saw was not silver but gold. I dropped the sack and reached into the water to lift out a nugget the size of a walnut. I held it to the light, then bit it. The piece was soft as gold. I searched further upstream and found another lump. Trembling, I scouted and found three other pieces.

With my hand full of gold, I knew I'd found a lode and my fortune. No one has suggested there is gold in Carolina. The Spanish have quested for gold much farther west. I sat in the leaves and examined the nuggets. I know well that gold will make people insane. I had no shovel to dig, no dish to pan, only my hands. And I mean to complete my mission for the Lord Proprietors. But I marked the spot, west of the Saponi, and will return. I will carry the nuggets back to London to trade for equipment, and later delve here on my own. At present I have no horse, and my only sustenance is what I can glean or snare from the forest, but I'm wealthy, because of my discovery. Where there are three or four nuggets there will be more. I'll outfit an expedition, and tell no one of the location.

August 4, 1711. The hunter warned me of rattlesnakes, and I've seen many beside rocks or logs. But all raised their tails and blurred an admonition, then uncoiled and writhed away into the brush. But today I came to a great windfall trunk, too long to go around. I sat on the log and put my left foot over, then heard the buzz, and before I could withdraw my leg, the pit viper struck above my boot and clung. I had to draw the head out of my flesh and fling the fiend away. Rolling up my trouser leg, I saw the two marks. After a few seconds the leg began to ache worse than ten hornet stings. The spot blanched, then grew red and hot, and later blue-green. I thought I would faint, but didn't.

Far in the wilderness I tried to think of remedies. The aborigines would know what to do. There must be a potion to counteract the venom. If the Indian was following me maybe he would come to my aid. "Help," I called, and shouted louder to the hills, "Help me!" I yelled, but echoes were my only answer. Surely there were Tuscaroras, or Catawbas, or Cherokees within hearing, but the forest was still, except for squirrel chatter. The hunter would know what to do, but he was far to the east.

I'd heard of sucking poison from a snakebite, but that had to be done immediately, and besides, I couldn't reach the spot on the side of my leg with my mouth, and too much time had already elapsed. I'd also heard of cutting the site and bleeding out the venom. With my knife I slit the skin around the fang marks and blood streamed.

As the toxin surged through my veins I grew light-headed. First there was pain, followed by numbness, as the venom killed feeling. The numbness spread through my limbs. I sat on the log and remembered my father's warning. He'd foreseen the dangers of the wilderness, of my passion for adventure and exploration. So far, I've survived. Can I outlive this also?

I rested on the blowdown tree, waiting for my mind to clear. Venom fogged my brain. I tried to recall my mission here in the New World, but the purpose mingled with my father's cautioning. A red streak began to crawl up my leg as the poison spread. I felt a new kind of pain. What would happen when the venom reached my heart? Or had it already touched my heart, because the organ fluttered and raced? And my thoughts were lost in smoke.

Sir, it's time to stir forward, I exhorted myself. Remember your pledge to the Lord Proprietors. You must not countenance defeat. I would cut a stick to use as a cane to avoid placing too much weight on the left leg. But holding the stick meant carrying the sack with my right hand, with no spelling, no relief.

I cut the stalk of a young hickory, and lifted the sack over my right shoulder, and struggled through the trees, following the river from a distance. The river would take me to the higher hills, and the rosary of mountains.

What is a man but his accomplishments, or lack of accomplishments? I muttered as I limped ahead. The ground was growing steeper. I leaned on trees for support and climbed. My left boot grew tighter, for the leg had swelled. I could not bend to inspect the leg without dropping the sack, but felt the enlargement under the trouser, the heat of pain.

As I climbed, the river dropped below. There was no choice but to climb, for otherwise I'd have to swing far around the acclivity, away from the river. I pushed myself, and recognized another purpose in ascending the hill: from the top I might survey the land ahead, and understand the territory to be crossed.

It was with the greatest effort that I resumed the climb, only to find the most forbidding cliff before me. The rock was decorated with moss and lichens, in many shades of green and gray. The cliff was high as a castle, with soaring battlements in two towers, with a kind of valley between. Unless I might ascend to the top I couldn't survey the land ahead.

I set the sack down and dropped my stick. The only way to reach the top was to crawl up the crotch gutter between the towers and hope one tower was accessible. As I began, I found the moss so slick I had to use elbows and knees as well as hands and toes for traction. With much effort, I achieved the summit, ignoring the pain of the snakebite and bruised elbows. But when I lifted my eyes over the top of the left tower, my labors were rewarded.

To the west I saw higher hills and a valley in haze as in a dream. And beyond the valley blue ridges rose one behind another, and farther still peaks loomed purple and the most distant seemed to merge with the vault of sky. It was another world, the hunting ranges of the Cherokees. I knew I must go there; to reach those summits would be the consummation of my mission. Those mountains were the reason I'd taken on the assignment. I must take their measure and return with my report. All my efforts will be justified, but I'll not mention the gold.

As I lay on the ledge and studied the remoteness ahead stretching far to the edge of heaven, I congratulated myself. I'd persisted, and it was my discovery. No doubt the Spanish had been there before me, coming from the south and west. But they'd not held it. I'd come from the Atlantic colonies, Protestant colonies, to establish claim, and report boundaries and latitude. I could rest there relieved that my errand had been half accomplished.

In the meantime, I had to descend the cliff and find a place of refuge where I might heal from the wound of the serpent. It might be days or weeks before I could recover strength and continue and complete my assignment. I surveyed the valley ahead for any meadow or clearing, any sign of habitation. The forest appeared unbroken to the farthest ravines and spurs of ridges. It was only when I dropped my sight to the cliff below that I discovered what appeared to be the entrance to a cavity. The opening looked out above the river. Could it be accessed?

With great effort I descended from the tower, slipping once and bruising a hip. But I made it to my bag and stick, and worked my way along a shelf in the cliff to the cave. The entrance faced west. By the time I reached the mouth I was exhausted. I thought I might be the first human to discover the cavern, but noticed pictures inscribed on the rock, what appeared to be runes or hieroglyphics. The natives had been there, maybe tribes long before the Cherokees and Catawbas.

Before entering the cave, I looked for snakes. My leg throbbed and I longed to lie down. There were leaves and sticks on the ledge, and with my flint and steel I struck a small fire to comfort me. Smoke rose and something flapped out of the entrance, brushing my head. After the first, others swooshed from the dark. One, overcome by smoke, fell on my leg. It was a small bat.

I lay in the mouth of the cavern and looked over the shelf at the rising land to the west where I must go. But first I would sleep and heal. The sun declined already over the many peaks and shadows advanced from the nearer hills. The ache in my legs had moved to my chest and into my whole body. My lips were dry. It was only as I lay down that I recalled what I needed most: I suffered a fever and had no water. I had nothing to drink but tears, salty tears. There could be no water in the high cave. I'd lost my bottle. Any spring would be far below. I would die without water.

I lay with lips stuck together and throat parched, needing sleep, needing an anodyne for the pain, needing water. A figure appeared against the sunset. The feather in his hair told me he was a native. The figure handed me a bowl of water and I drank, and then the bowl and the figure vanished. Had I dreamed? Was I delirious? And yet I tasted the water and felt its coolness in my body. Was it a miracle, like the ravens feeding Elijah in the wilderness?

With water in me I lay in the last rays of sunset and slept.

In the morning I still had the fever and aches in my body, but retrieved the notebook from the sack and recorded this. I must consider and plan. And I need water again. I'm high above the river and not sure I can climb down this embankment. Will I be able to walk on the left leg? My task is less than half complete. Clearly the Indian who brought me water, if he is real, has been following me all these days. Everything I've done has been observed. Is he Cherokee or Tuscarora? Is he reporting my actions? Why did he bring me the water? I'm burning with thirst and fever and pain.

August 5, 1711. This morning I thought I heard water dripping inside the cave. Was I imagining the sound? I made another fire, and with a burning stick limped into the cavern with one hand holding to the wall. There were bones on the floor, as though hunters had brought their kills here, or animals had come here to die. There were large bones that must have belonged to bears, or even bigger animals, skeletons ten feet long, or more, as though from an age of giants. I saw human bones also, skulls and ribs. This is a mystery, for why are so many bones here, in this cave inside a cliff?

I paused to listen, and edged further toward the drip, stepping carefully to avoid the skeletons. Looking at my feet to keep from falling, I didn't notice at first the drawings on the walls, but when I glanced up saw pictures, made with charcoal, of animals, and human figures throwing spears, and circles like the sun and moon. Someone had sketched dozens of images, colored with clay or berry juice, like pictures in a chapel. No doubt natives are the artists. But the drawings look ancient, from another era or dispensation. I was looking at prehistory, so old the designs were crumbling.

But my attention turned to the sound of water. I held the torch forward and discovered a seepage from the rocks, a trickle that soaked right out of the wall and dripped to the floor where the dribble drained into a crevice. I held the torch in my left hand and filled the right palm and drank, then drank again. A dozen times I gulped from my hand. But what I needed was a container to carry a supply to the entrance. Otherwise I'd have to stumble back over the bones again and again.

There was nothing in my pockets. I looked behind me. A dusty skeleton lay within reach. With hesitation I lifted the skull into the light and rinsed it as best I could, then held it under the leak until it overflowed. With great care, holding the torch in my right hand, the skull in the left, I staggered to the entrance, spilling half of my treasure.

Today I sat at the entry, sipping from the skull as the swelling in my leg grew worse. The venom rots my flesh, and the place where I cut the skin over the bite is infected. The flesh, once red, grows black and green, though the pain lessens. Instead, I know a dizziness, the floating of a fever. Is the aborigine still watching me? If so, he sees I have water in my unusual bowl. The cup is also my memento mori.

What am I doing here? My father's voice speaks as from the sky. What would you do, John, with your escape into the wilderness? What message do you bring for the aborigines? For the pagans? No, my survey is for the Lord Proprietors, for the Queen, for England. I must complete the assignment. These notes will be the testimony.

I looked over the valley, over the hills, at the ranges to the west, where mountains multiply themselves, at the far ravines and millions of trees, at the sweeping rivers that gather from the springs of the watersheds, at the cloud shadows moving easily over uneven terrain, and saw trails becoming highways and forests yielding to fields and pastures. From my high vantage point, I watched groves translate to towns and cities. Towers and domes rose over the streams. Villages of the natives gave way to foundries and churches, replacing bark huts. Streets teemed, with citizens hawking wares, and warehouses and counting houses replaced hunters' camps. The world grows near and then far. I wish I had my telescope.

The wonderful vista of civilization stretched over the primeval wilderness, and I felt the joy of triumph, the reward for my surveying. Until I looked longer and closer, and saw among the alleys and avenues, pickpockets, thieves, husbands beating wives, murderers, priests preying on choir boys, embezzlers, liars, prostitutes. In place of forests, the streets were sewers of mud, manure, rotting refuse from butcher shops, abattoirs, hospitals of mental disorders. The future was also a familiar country.

The vision lasted only seconds, but it stunned me. For I could see clearly one possible consequence of my survey. The consummation of my mission was also a prospect of horror. Civilization polluted the primeval.

As I write this a shadow falls on the page, and I find the same native standing before me. He stares into my eyes. He wears a feather and his face and chest are painted red and black. He holds a spear at his side, but makes no gesture. His stare is rude. I try to speak, but find no words. The hallucination of the future has vanished, and there is nothing but woodlands and mountains behind him.

When I look up again he's gone, as quickly as he materialized. But I do not believe the warrior is an apparition. I think he wants me to know he follows and monitors my progress. He wants me to remember I'm observed.

My leg swells more than ever. I must find my way back to the seepage for the skull is empty. The death's-head lies before me like a tortoise shell. I will take a torch from the fire and stumble into the dark again, through the illustrations of bison, panthers, hunters with spears. But first I'll wait and rest. Why should I hurry? The drip will not go away. It keeps time like a perpetual clock, plink, plink, plink, the great clock inside the mountain, in flowers, in stars.

With the swelling greater than ever, I expect to feel more pain. But instead, I feel a faraway numbness, as if I'd taken laudanum, as if my flesh were floating in the womb. I'll rest here a while, before continuing my survey. This notebook is my testament. The rock I lean against is soft as a pillow. From the sack I take the lumps of gold and turn them one by one in the sun. They are my securities. I feel neither weight nor sorrow. The valley before me is glorious as an endless garden. I'm utterly happy, too sleepy to write more.

War No More

SOME MIGHT CALL ME A COWARD, a deserter, even a traitor. But looking back on those terrible days, I wouldn't have done anything different after Shiloh. I did what had to be done and would again if circumstances were the same. There is even Biblical sanction for my actions, come to that, events I live, and live again, replaying them in memory.

Back in the awful summer of 1862, after Shiloh and the advance on Corinth, and then the battle of Corinth, I lived for almost a year in the attic of an old plantation house, in heat that could suffocate or broil you, and in cold that turned your bones to glass. For company I had bats, an old spinning wheel, a rocking horse, tobacco leaves, wasps, a trunk full of papers and hidden silver and a wedding dress, empty jars, a pitcher, old letters, a globe, yellowed newspapers, half an encyclopedia, a telescope, a moth-eaten top hat, Venetian blinds, a whip, fishing tackle, a chest of drawers, a chamber pot, a pallet, a rusting lantern, a coil of rope, a large indigo snake that fed on mice, two bottles of laudanum, and a mistress from Ohio.

How I got into the attic is not an unusual story in wartime. In the second advance in Mississippi, in the summer heat that made you crazy, I saw men I'd served with, eaten breakfast with, lose arms and legs, and heads, to cannon fire. Grapeshot hissed, a ball touched my left arm. Bodies lay around me, intestines spilled on the ground. I could smell blood and excrement in the smoke. Major Stokes ordered an advance, and Sergeant Enslow screamed the command. The blood and smoke made me throw up and I didn't crawl forward. Instead I groveled to the left, into a field or garden. Coughing and crying, I heaved along. There was no decision; it was made for me. On hands and knees I reached some woods. My eyes burned and streamed, and dirt and leaves stuck to my face.

What have you done, Dwight Williams? I said, hardly knowing what had happened. I'd deserted, and could face a rope or firing squad. I'd acted under an unconscious order. I soon stood and ran, leaving the screams, groans, and boom-vowels of the battlefield behind me. Tears blurred my sight, and I banged into tree trunks, scratched my legs on briars, stung my eyes with twigs.

I ran bent over, as if following a voice I couldn't hear, stumbling mile after mile, to escape the rope, the shame, the disgrace to my family in New York.

It was almost dark when I emerged from the woods at the edge of a cornfield, hands and face bloody and swollen with scratches and bug bites. My legs were ready to buckle, and my chest sore from gulping smoke and humid air. I fell and tried to think. There were lights in a large white house ahead, and a fire in the backyard. Figures stirred around the fire and I could smell cooking. Behind the big house stretched a line of cabins, slave quarters I guessed. Light shone from some of the cabin doors. A windlass over a well was visible behind the big house.

It was then thirst hit me, the ache in the mouth and throat, a stiffness, when you're willing to give your life for a cup of cool water, or even warm water. The sweating and panting had drained me. But I was a blue-belly, a Yankee, and knew the danger. I could be shot as an enemy, or thief. I lay on the ground as the stars appeared and noise around the big house subsided. Silhouettes drew water from the well; lights in the shacks vanished. The fire in the yard shrank to a glow and then died.

Stepping through rows of cotton, I advanced, swinging wide around the slave cabins. No one seemed to stir in the yard. I didn't try to draw water with the noisy windlass, and the bucket on the rim was empty. My hope was to find a pail of water on the back porch or in the kitchen. A dog walked up to me and whimpered. I held out my hand and it didn't bark. The screen door to the porch groaned a little when I opened it.

I struck a match and saw a wooden bucket with a dipper. I filled the dipper and brought it to my lips, but just as I drank the precious liquid a figure carrying a lantern appeared in the shadows of the yard.

"Miss Alice, is that you?" a man said.

The door into the kitchen was open on the right and I slipped through, smelling the smoke and sweat on my uniform. The man carrying the lantern opened the porch door and stepped inside. "Miss Alice, is that you?" he said again.

I eased through a door to the left and found my hand on the newel post of stairs. Instinctively I held to the railing and climbed the steps, reaching the landing just as the man with the lantern entered the room. Gripping the bannister, I felt my way to the second flight.

"Miss Alice," the voice called from below, and the lantern began mounting the stairs.

What a fool I'd been to take the stairs. I should have run back outside, for now I was trapped. Even if the man with the lantern was armed, I could have fled into the dark. There was nothing to do but climb higher. Holding to the railing and moving quietly, I reached the second floor in the dark. The lantern didn't follow.

To my horror, a door opened and a woman with long hair, holding a candle, stepped out. I expected a scream, but there was no scream. She held the light up to get a better look at me, and whispered "Come." She led me up the next flight of stairs. Slowly and quietly I followed, holding to the railing. She smelled of soap and cologne, scents I hadn't enjoyed for more than a year. When we reached the third floor she pointed to a door at the end of a hallway. With nervous steps I followed. She opened the door to a closet hiding steep steps to the attic. "Quiet" she said, pointing up the steps, and handed me the candlestick.

"How will you get down?" I said.

"I know my own house." There was a hint of a Northern accent in her voice. In a second she was gone and the closet door shut. I climbed the steps into the attic.

Two things overwhelmed me as I stepped onto the upper floor: the heat and the smell of old wood and dust, of paper and tobacco. Boards groaned as I moved. The space was filled with things broken or no longer wanted, things too good to be thrown away, forgotten. I made my way to a louvered window latched in place. With some effort I got it open and luxuriated in the slightly cooler night air. There were voices downstairs, then all was quiet.

Almost too exhausted to stand, I looked for something to collapse on. A dusty bedstead had no mattress. There were quilts and blankets stacked against a chest of drawers. As quietly as possible I cleared a space and spread three quilts for a pallet. I didn't need any cover. Before dropping, I opened the window at the other end of the loft to make a cross-breeze. I must have been asleep before my head touched the folded-blanket pillow.

•

It was the lady of the night before who wakened me. She placed a chamber pot and a pitcher of water at the top of the stairs. Then she returned with a pail containing bread and a boiled egg, and blackberries. "I'm sorry I don't have more to offer," she said. "Half the servants are gone. I freed them when my husband left for the war. Now I have few to work the cotton fields. Those who stayed keep the garden, one cow and chickens."

Miss Alice appeared to be in her late thirties. She had light brown hair and a remarkably beautiful face, with sensitive "French" features, and fine skin. Her figure was robust. She explained she would empty the chamber pot into her own and pretend the rations were for herself; but even so the servants would soon guess she was hiding someone in the loft, even if they pretended not to notice. She would have to trust the butler Alfred, and the cook Sarah. She spoke in a very low voice. I drank out of the pitcher as she talked, and began to munch the bread and egg. While I ate, she poured water from the pitcher into a small glass hidden beneath a box, and took a bottle from the same hiding place. Adding drops from the bottle to the water, she drank the mixture hurriedly and replaced the glass and bottle. I later found the bottle contained laudanum.

"The servants must not know where this is hidden."

"I won't tell."

"This war is a nightmare," she said. "It's the punishment for slavery."

I thought it unusual that a Southern lady on a plantation would speak so bitterly about the institution she lived by. Soon after Mississippi had seceded, both her husband and son had joined the new army, she told me. Her daughter had married and lived in New Orleans. She'd been left alone to manage the house and land. After she freed the slaves only half a dozen remained to help her in the house and fields.

Thus began my life in the attic of Pemberley, the Wilson manor house. I learned that Miss Alice had grown up in Ohio and met her husband, Horace Wilson, at a ball in Cincinnati. Mr. Wilson had served as an officer in the Black Hawk War. Like so many young girls, she was impressed by his uniform and graciousness. Though uneasy about slavery, she had accepted the way of life in Mississippi. "I have no right to complain," she said. "I made the choice myself." She paused and looked at me. "The young don't understand some choices are forever, and Mr. Wilson is an honorable man. What seemed an interim became a life."

In the isolation of the farm in wartime she missed her son and daughter. The laudanum helped.

In the days that followed, as I sweated in the attic, avoiding wasps and spiders, hoping for a breeze from the louvered windows, I sometimes heard cannon fire in the distance. Miss Alice knew little about the war news, but what she did learn she shared with me. I shuddered to remember I was a deserter.

What I'd done in the rage of battle could never be undone. At the moment of decision, I'd acted as though under mesmeric control, as if I could not have acted otherwise. Yet any court-martial would hold me guilty.

There were old books in the attic, many falling apart. Some were in foreign languages. One was a history of the American Revolution. I found underneath the pile an old Bible. The leather covers had been eaten by mice or insects. The pages were yellow and brittle and tore easily. I had a lamp Miss Alice had brought up, but it was too dangerous to light at night until after midnight. I preferred to read by daylight at one of the windows. Holding the fragile book to the light I studied the stories learned in Sunday School years ago and forgotten. Maybe it was the remorse I suffered, but never before had I realized how vivid the stories of Moses and David and all the others were, stories of rape and incest, war and death. Yet the *Psalms* were soothing, and *Ecclesiastes* wise and sad. But when I came to a passage in *Micah* 4:3, I understood what had happened to me that day at Corinth: "they shall beat their swords into plowshares, and their spears into pruninghooks: nation shall not lift up sword against nation, neither shall they learn war anymore."

It was that last phrase that touched me: *neither shall they learn war anymore*. The word *learn* was so unusual. I kept replaying the scenes at Shiloh and Corinth in my mind, and my escape into the woods, my life in the attic. The word made some sense of it all. I'd been a school teacher, but I would not *learn* war anymore. As I read the passage again tears threaded down my cheeks. I was trapped in a boiling attic, and a lady had to carry out my waste every morning. I had to wash with a rag in a pan of water. But the ancient words comforted me and explained what I had done.

As the weather began to cool, there came several days of tragedy. First, Miss Alice informed me that her husband had been killed in a cornfield at a place called Sharpsburg or Antietam on September 17. It had taken a month for the news to reach her. Just days later she learned that her son Jacob had died of typhoid or typhus in Virginia. And weeks after that she was informed that her daughter Wilma in New Orleans had died in childbirth. The baby has been stillborn. My attempts to console her sounded empty and absurd.

As it cooled in the attic I closed the two windows and wrapped myself in quilts and blankets. When Miss Alice came up to the loft she was sullen and distracted. The rations she brought shrank to beans and corn bread, except for a boiled egg on Sundays. She spoke little and informed me that her mother, an invalid who lived in one of the rooms on the second floor, had died and would be buried in the woods nearby. "Maybe this is more punishment for slavery," she whispered.

I tried again to find words of sympathy, but there were none. A preacher would say that God works in mysterious ways, and knows more than mortal humans can understand, but I couldn't repeat such glib assurances. All I could think of were those words from *Micah* and I recited them.

"You are my only comfort now," Miss Alice said. To distract herself from the terrible sorrows, she asked about my life before the war. I told her I was a teacher in a place called Geneva, New York, that I had grown up along the Erie Canal. As a youth I'd learned to guide barges pulled by horses or mules along the waterway, to close the gates of locks, and when the locks were filled or emptied, continue the journey. I described barges passing each other. She asked why I had become a teacher. I told her that in a financial Panic that was the only job I could find. Every village needed a teacher.

"Mr. Williams, you are a man of parts," she said.

I described the Finger Lakes region, the gorges and waterfalls, the mills turned by water power, the hills smoothed by glaciers thousands of years ago, the Indian reservations. It was all I could think of, to make small talk. Her grief was too great to discuss.

I don't want you to misunderstand what I am about to say. We are all only human, and the body has it own needs, as the belly has its priorities, and the heart has it own hungers. But I noticed in the days after the torrent of tragedies how Miss Alice looked at me when she brought the water and victuals. It was a different kind of study. She had shown sympathy for my plight, for me, a fugitive and deserter. I was reminded of the way girls after a dance, or on moonlit nights in a buggy, might stare. She was a widow and I an ignorant young man of twenty-five. But even I, in my ignorance, knew that look was significant. At first I tried to ignore her stare, but it stirred me.

She was my hostess. I depended on her for every crumb I ate and every sip of water. I could not afford to offend her. One afternoon she appeared at an unusual hour. The house was quiet. She looked into my eyes and said she was wearing nothing under her skirts. She opened her blouse and revealed generous breasts. I must tell you I no more made a decision there in the attic than I had at the battle at Corinth. My flesh had its own will and authority. What she said was true: she wore nothing under the long skirt.

We made love in a frantic way on the quilts, more passionate than I'd ever known before. There was no laughter, no teasing, no speaking. It was as though each of us was carried beyond ourselves to some other state. The war and many deaths served as a kind of philter. We meant no disrespect. It was life speaking to life in the presence of death, life so much threatened in a time of dying. Alice had lost everything: desire was her only tether to life.

Afterward we didn't speak, for there was nothing to say. We could understand what had happened, yet we were mystified by the intensity of it. The mistress of a plantation had given herself in a time of mourning to a twenty-five-year-old deserter who smelled of sweat. I will never forget until the hour of my death the look Alice gave me as she announced she wore nothing under her skirts. There was enthrallment in the stare, the elation of a million years of passion as nature paid its dues to the future, in the fever of desire. In that season of sorrow she'd helped me become a man, hopefully a wiser and better man.

After that visit in the afternoon her regular visits continued, usually in the morning, before the stirring in the house below. But when she appeared in the afternoon, while the servants were in the fields or backyard at other work, there was that look, and I knew the visit would be sweet and longer. She no longer had to tell me there was nothing under her dress, but would begin loosening her top. She was a bigger woman than the girls I'd loved at home, and more direct in her desire.

After we made love one afternoon we lay quiet for several minutes, and then she spoke in a low voice of her childhood in Ohio, about her parents' move from Pennsylvania to western Ohio, about her education in a small red schoolhouse. She asked if I knew why most schoolhouses were painted red. I shook my head. "To show they are not churches," she said. Churches were always white to show purity and piety. Red suggested the worldliness of learning. She described the country dances she'd attended as a girl, and the ball in Cincinnati where she met Mr. Wilson. "When a girl falls in love there's no reasoning with her," she said. She'd married at the age of fifteen.

Alice asked if I had a sweetheart at home, if I enjoyed dancing, if I attended church, and did I intend to return to teaching after the war. I told her I would be disgraced as a deserter. No one would ever hire me to teach again. "There are other professions, and other places," she said. One question she asked led to a conversation we continued for several of our afternoons. "Where would you like to live, if you could live anywhere?"

"On the first floor."

"No, I mean any place, any state."

We talked about Upstate New York, the valleys of Ohio, Florida, the virtues of city-dwelling versus country living, mountain versus flat country. It was a dialogue we prolonged for weeks, describing places we'd known, places we'd read about or heard about, and places we imagined. It was a way of avoiding her many sorrows, and my shame and remorse. It was also an attempt to distract each other, in our unusual circumstances, by thinking of distant havens.

"I want to live somewhere the war doesn't reach, and where slavery was never practiced," Alice said.

"Maine?" I offered. I knew there had been slaves in most of the Northern states.

"California," she whispered. California had become a state in 1850 on the condition it would be a Free state. After that we discussed everything we knew about California, its harbors and missions, its deserts and High Sierra, the Coast Ranges, the palm trees and giant redwoods, the gold fields.

"It's two thousand miles away," I said.

"A journey begins with a single step."

Such talk was a way of diverting us from the horror around us, the boom of distant cannon, the rotting fields, the hunger. It was a fantasy suggesting that some day the war might actually end. Alice brought a coil of rope to the attic and laid it near the western window.

"Is that to hang myself?" I said.

"If a patrol comes to arrest you, maybe you can escape."

•

One day in December I heard horses. Opening a louver a little I saw mounted graybacks approaching. Soon I heard voices and chickens cackling, and when the soldiers rode away they carried sacks that held Alice's hens. I would have no more boiled eggs for breakfast.

Later in the same month another column of graybacks appeared and shot the last hog and carted it away. There would be no bacon that winter. On Christmas morning Alice brought me the usual cornbread and beans, but there was a sprig of holly with bright red berries. She asked me to read in a quiet voice the story of the first Christmas from *Luke* chapters one and two.

"You have the voice of a schoolteacher," she said.

"I have the voice of a fugitive."

The next time I heard loud voices I peeked from the window and saw a line of blue-clad soldiers approaching on the long driveway. Ice dropped through my bones to the soles of my feet. I'd been dreading their appearance. With a blanket wrapped around my shoulders I shuddered.

"You have a deserter here, named Private Williams," Major Stokes shouted.

Alice's voice answered, but I couldn't make out her words.

Guessing they might search the house, I covered the chamber pot and breakfast dish with a quilt, and slid the chest of drawers out far enough for me to hide behind, then squeezed into the space. Once the soldiers entered the house, the walls echoed with heavy steps, loud voices, and the ring of spurs.

"Lady, if you're harboring a deserter, you will be hanged and your house burned." Doors slammed and walls were hit the way a doctor thumps on a chest. Pots and pans fell, boots banged on stairs, wardrobes were overturned, and glass shattered, either pitchers or lamps.

"There's a report you're hiding a deserter," the major shouted.

"No, sir," Alice answered.

Closet doors were opened.

"That is my wedding silver," Alice said.

"It will be your contribution to the Union."

Metal rang on the floor.

Heavy steps mounted to the third story, just below my hiding place. Bottles and jars were swept to the floor. My breath shortened, and my lips grew dry and stuck together.

"Look in the attic," a voice snarled. It was Sergeant Enslow. The door to the steep steps was opened, and risers squeaked. I could smell the soldiers, the stink of sweat, campfires, horses, unwashed bodies, the stench of boots worn day after day, aromas I knew well.

"Bring me a lantern," the sergeant called. When the light was brought I saw shadows play on the walls around me. I shrank into myself and tried not to breathe. My heart thundered so I thought surely the soldiers could hear it.

"Look here," the sergeant said, "a real long rifle."

"We're not supposed to loot." The two soldiers began laughing. Steps banged to the far side of the attic, then returned. Things were rattled and thrown down. "I'm taking this old telescope," the other soldier said.

"What would you do with a telescope?"

"I'd watch a grayback taking a shit."

They found the silver hidden in the trunk.

Steps approached the chest of drawers. I was certain they'd discovered me. I would try to jump out a window rather than be taken to be tortured and hanged.

"Ain't nothing here but women's underwear."

"You could wear that at night, Tankersley."

"Kiss my royal ass."

Just when I was sure they'd spotted me, they walked away, and their boots banged on the steps. Their clothes were so rancid they hadn't smelled the urine in the piss pot. There was another crash below. Alice later told me they gathered all her silver in a sack and took it.

"You hide a deserter, I'll come back with a noose for both of you," the major called, as he mounted his horse.

I'd been so scared I was sweaty and trembling. It took me hours to calm myself. The soldiers had searched within three feet of my shivering flesh. I watched them ride away from the west window, and knew if I'd used the rope the soldiers would have shot me before I touched the ground. There was no escape from my lair.

The portions of beans and bread Alice brought shrank further. It was all she had. I learned the soldiers had knocked out the back of the corncrib and trampled the spilled ears in the mud with their horses. Soon even cornmeal would be scarce.

•

It must have been late February or early March when I first noticed the ghost. The sound always came in the night, when the attic was dark as a coal mine. There was rustling in the corner where so many pieces of old furniture were stacked. Something moved with a dry rasping noise. I thought at first it must be mice. Mice came and went in the loft; in warmer weather they seemed to disappear. But these sounds were eerie, like small chains dragged over boards. When I mentioned the sounds to Alice she said, "Have you seen the ghost yet?"

"What ghost?"

She told me the story of her husband's aunt. In the days when the family first arrived from North Carolina, just after the Chickasaws and Choctaws were expelled, the lovely Jenny Wilson became engaged to a planter named Santis from Louisiana. There were plans for a grand wedding and a honeymoon in New Orleans. The newlyweds would travel by carriage to Memphis and by steamboat to the Crescent City. Jenny spent months preparing her trousseau and wedding dress, her fetching nightclothes.

Two days before the nuptials, an anonymous letter arrived saying, "I am the woman carrying your fiancé's baby." Jenny was stunned but said little. She had led a sheltered life. Brother and mother tried to comfort her, explained the letter might be a cruel prank. The morning of the wedding she could not be found. Santis appeared, but the bride had vanished. The house was searched and the surrounding countryside scoured. Finally, Jenny's brother, Alice's father-in-law, remembered the attic, and found her hanging from a beam by the train of her wedding dress. Alice showed me the timber to which the fabric and been tied.

"Sometimes her footsteps have been heard on the stairs, and the creak of her weight on the beam" Alice said.

I told her I'd heard no creak of the beam except in high wind, nor any steps on the stairs, and I didn't believe in ghosts.

"If you spot the ghost let me know. I want to see if there's a family resemblance."

Alice was attempting to be cheerful. More of the remaining servants had disappeared after the visit of the Union company. There were only Alfred, who had been the butler, and Sarah, who helped with the cleaning and cooking. Until a new garden could be planted and harvested we would all be on meager rations.

I was startled one night by the peculiar sound underfoot. I jumped and the sound stopped. I lit a match and saw nothing but the dusty floor. Whatever made the noise was apparently invisible. Yet I'd heard the movement distinctly, right under me. It was maybe half an hour later when I noticed the disturbance again, to my side and retreating. I struck another match but saw nothing.

For about a week I listened to the odd sounds of rasping, but whenever I lit a match there was nothing. If it was a ghost it was perfectly transparent, the kind of ghost that made noise but could not be seen, the kind called up at seances. Once I said, "Who are you? Show yourself." But there was no answer. "I'm not afraid of you," I bragged.

One night the racket came from the corner where the old furniture and chest of drawers were stacked. I lit a candle, determined to follow the noise and finally expose its source. Quietly as I could, I stepped around the junk and paraphernalia, trying not to rattle jars or metal frames. The noise rose into the clutter of old clothes and dusty chairs. Something moved and a crumpled curtain stirred. Holding my breath, I stepped closer. Whatever it was pushed against the cloth and moved behind a piece of heavy velour.

"Show yourself," I ordered, and held the candle forward, and just at that moment two gleaming eyes appeared, reflecting the candlelight, and a tongue licked the air. I froze as the nose of a giant black snake stretched out of the rags and poured itself to the floor. It must have been six or seven feet long. I realized why I hadn't been able to see it before: it was catching mice in the space between the ceiling below and the floor of the attic. The snake was sleek and well-fed. My companion in the attic was not a ghost but a long, indigo snake.

I wondered if such a snake could be killed and eaten, though I had no inclination to kill or eat it. As I watched, the serpent disappeared into the clutter of dust and furniture.

When I told Alice what I'd discovered about the "ghost," she said the snake must be killed. She would have no snake in her house. I explained that the indigo reptile was valuable to catch mice and rats, and harmless to humans.

For several days I didn't see the viper again, and then the noises under the floor returned, and kept me company throughout the night.

In the attic, at the level of oaks and catalpa trees, I heard many songbirds. I listened to robins and warblers, blue jays and cardinals, buntings and mockingbirds. Because I had so much time, I became more literate in birdcalls. I'd listened to the songsters before, but not closely. I became aware of a whole new world of communication in the air and sky, among the tree limbs, love calls, warning calls, joyful expressions. Crows in the distance sounded their alarms. Sometimes a hawk whistled. A dove hushed the morning. A bobwhite chirped. In the evening whippoorwills answered themselves beyond the barn.

I explained my new literacy in birdcalls to Alice, but she was too worried to take much interest. "What will we do when the cornmeal runs out?" she said. Her cheeks were hollow, and I noticed some gray strands in her hair. She gave me the look less often when she visited, nor did she mention she wore nothing under her skirts. The laudanum was gone, and she complained of headaches and nerves.

It was in late March when she brought me boiled greens, which she called "creesies." They had an unusual smell, flavored with vinegar.

"Will they poison me?" I asked.

"It's nothing but wild mustard." She explained that local people ate creesies with vinegar in spring to thin their blood, a tonic to prepare them for warmer weather.

"I wish we had boiled eggs to go with the greens." She explained that the servants often ate a little branch clay in spring for the same purpose. I got used to the mustard greens with cornbread, and then shoots of pokeweed, also seasoned with vinegar.

•

Soon it grew warm in the attic again. Grayback patrols came by the house to drink from the well, but there was nothing more in the yard or barn for them to steal. The chickens, cow, and horses had long ago been requisitioned. Some of the graybacks pilfered through the house, but didn't try the attic. I hid behind the chest of drawers, but they never came there. Alice said there was a terrible battle in progress at Vicksburg, but she didn't know how it would turn out.

We talked more about California, about the palm trees, about the ocean, and the rich soil of the central valley. "I've never seen the ocean," Alice said. "Mr. Wilson promised to take me to Paris, but then the war broke out."

"California is only two thousand miles away," I said, and we both laughed.

One morning Alice announced that both the remaining servants, Alfred and Sarah, had gone, disappeared in the night. "I can't blame them," she said. "They have my blessing to find freedom. I just wish they'd stayed a little longer."

A thought occurred to her. "No need for you to stay up here. You can move down and sleep in a bed." I hugged her and gave her a kiss. My exile in the attic was over.

Just then we heard the squeak of saddles and voices below. "Oh, my God!" Alice groaned. She hurried down the steps and ran to the first floor. A door slammed.

There was shouting. I watched from the west window. Major Stokes, still on his horse, said, "Mrs. Wilson, I warned you about harboring a deserter."

"I harbor no one," Alice said.

Sergeant Enslow stepped forward and slapped Alice so hard she spun around and almost fell.

"We have all day," the major said. "Where is he hiding, in the barn, in the well, in the potato hole?"

"I hide no one," Alice said, with a hand on her burning cheek. Her nose bled.

"We know better from one of your servants," the major said. "Tell us where he is, in a secret closet, the cellar, the attic, in a tunnel?"

Alice wiped the blood from her upper lip with her handkerchief. The sergeant was about to hit her again, but the major told him to stop. "You're hiding someone from us, Mrs. Wilson. Let's see where you keep him."

Sergeant Enslow grabbed her dress on either shoulder and tore it down to the waist. She stood before the company with her breasts exposed, naked to the hips. Alice attempted to cover herself with her hands.

"Now, let's start again," the major said. "You will tell us where the traitor is hiding or we'll go further." He nodded toward the company.

Alice bowed in shame, and turned away from the men.

"We'll burn this place to the ground," the major said, "starting with the barn."

A detail of men made twists of straw and lit them to throw into the barn. From my perch I saw smoke rise from the door and windows of the barn. As the flames reached higher, into the hayloft, a man jumped from the loft door and ran toward the field. He wore rags of a butternut uniform. Neither Alice nor I knew a Confederate deserter had hidden in the barn.

"Take him!" the major shouted. All the blue-bellies turned toward the running man. Some raised their rifles; others gave chase. All eyes followed the fleeing deserter. Alice saw her chance and ran desperately around the house, out of view of the soldiers, and stumbled across the spring garden into the woods. I watched her from the east window until she disappeared.

Meanwhile the Confederate fugitive zigzagged across last year's cotton field as bullets picked puffs of dust around him. He must have been hit on a leg, for soon he began limping, dragging one foot as he lurched. Before he could make it to the trees he fell, and didn't stir again.

Only then did the major and sergeant remember Alice, but when they turned she was gone.

"We will find you!" the major called. "And when we find you, you will serve my men." The major ordered the company to search the woodshed, the outhouses, the summer kitchen, the corncrib. The barn roared and flames reached into the sky. The sergeant and three men plundered the first floor and cellar of the house and found only a few bottles of wine. They mounted to the second and third floors, but didn't try the attic. They took a clock from the mantel of the parlor and looked for silver. They seized a hat that had belonged to Mr. Wilson.

By then it was late afternoon. The sergeant suggested they set the house ablaze, but the major said, no, they could stay the night here. Besides, Mrs. Wilson might come out of hiding, or even the deserter. The company cooked their supper in the yard and tromped into the bedrooms on the second and third floors. They carried all the bottles of wine from the cellar. Fights broke out over the wine and who would sleep in beds or on the floor. They'd not slept under a roof for many months. I heard men pissing on the floor and out windows.

"Where do you reckon that fucking bitch went?"

"How far can she carry them big tits?"

"I'd just like to get my hands on both of them."

It seemed the house would never quiet. There was laughter and angry voices, glass breaking, things thrown from windows, farting. I recalled how much I hated camp life. Hours passed like years. It must have been midnight, or one a.m., when, finally, the house was still.

I tied the rope to a beam above the west window, and let the end of the rope down, hoping it would reach the ground and not hit the wall. Last, I thought of what I should carry and crammed matches and two candles in my pocket, a paring knife Alice had given me. I slipped on boots that had belonged to Mr. Wilson, and leather gloves.

It was only after I climbed through the window, grasping the rope, that I saw the danger of swinging out and back, touching the wall with my feet. I would need to lower myself slowly down the rope, touching the wall as little as possible. I wrapped the rope around my thighs, and released it little by little, glad I had on the gloves.

There was snoring in the rooms. Once my knees knocked the wall and someone called out, 'Who's there?" But they must have gone back to sleep. Inch by inch I lowered myself toward the yard. But as I'd feared, the rope was too short. I came to the end, still ten or twelve feet above the ground. I hesitated, then unwrapped the rope from my thighs and dropped.

A pain burned through my right leg. I must have hit a rock or jar left there. I knelt in the grass hoping nothing was broken. Gradually the ache subsided. That was when I saw a light in the parlor window. Someone stirred, like they'd heard me fall. The window opened just a few feet away, and a lamp was held out the window. I pressed as close to the foundation as possible. It was the major holding the lamp, and he peered into the dark. He likely had left someone on guard duty, on the other side of the house, near the well. I held my breath. As moths gathered around the lamp the major withdrew and closed the window. His steps returned to the sofa.

To reach the woods I had to cross the old garden. Sticks and stalks rattled with each step. Once I broke a stick that must have been a tomato stake. The pop echoed off the house, and the sentry stepped around the corner of the building with his rifle raised. He didn't speak, but searched the dark, listened, then retreated.

When I reached the woods I saw the difficulty of making my way through trees and vines, with limbs jabbing my eyes. It would be nearly impossible without a light, and there was no moon. I could blind myself on a sharp branch. I struck a match but a voice said, "Put that out." I froze.

"It's me," Alice said.

I stood so quiet I could hear my own breathing.

"Where are you?" Alice called.

I almost spoke, but caught myself. Tears brimmed in both eyes. There were only the sounds of the forest, a twig dropped, an owl spoke faraway, a dog barked in the distance, a cricket nearby.

"Don't you want to travel to California with an old lady?" she said.

I put a hand to my mouth like a muzzle.

"We could travel together over mountains and rivers, away from war." Her voice broke.

After another minute she began to walk to the left, swishing limbs as she struggled to find a way in the dark.

Jack

Much as he loved the Dalmatian, Mark knew he was going to have to train him better. Jack had some bad habits that simply had to be broken. For one thing, the young dog knew no restraint in the display of affection. He would jump up on you and put his paws on your belly or chest and try to lick your face. This was especially annoying when his paws were wet or muddy and you were wearing good clothes. Last Sunday Jack had jumped on the preacher when he came for dinner and ruined his suit and tie. Mildred had tried to wash the stains out with a damp cloth with only limited success, and they'd given the preacher money for dry cleaning.

Even worse was Jack's habit of crowding around your ankles while you tried to walk. To show his enthusiasm and affection Jack would lean against your legs, and several times Mark had tripped over him and fallen. Mark was eighty-three and had arthritis, and was afraid of breaking a hip. It did no good to try to step around Jack, for the Dalmatian would anticipate your moves and jump in front of you again.

"Out of my way!" Mark would say. But instead of stepping back Jack pressed even closer, whimpering and yelping with excitement.

"That dog is going to put you in the hospital," Mildred liked to snap. "And then we know where you'll be put." Usually Mildred did not mention that Mark had been diagnosed with dementia, but sometimes she referred to his condition to make a point.

Many of Mark and Mildred's friends, those still alive, were already in nursing homes. More than anything Mark wanted to avoid such a facility. Someday he'd probably have to go there, but now he could still walk, and he could still work. He mowed his own grass with the riding mower, and he'd built a doghouse for Jack that had a window. That spring he'd even painted the porch, climbing up on the stepladder to reach the trim. There was no reason he couldn't go on living as he had for a while longer, whatever the doctor said. But a broken hip would put him in the hospital or rehab for months, and once there he might never be allowed to leave.

It was said that having a dog was good for the elderly. Caring for a dog was a rewarding responsibility, the kind that kept you alert and hopeful. The affection and loyalty of a dog made you feel better, more yourself. A lively and friendly pet helped fight depression, so common a threat of old age. Attention to a dog took the place of some of the things he'd lost. So many things that had always worked for him didn't any longer. And not just his equipment, which seemed to have curled up and gone to sleep and refuse to respond when called on, but also hearing and memory let him down just when he needed them most. And his eyes blurred things, even with glasses, sometimes. His balance wasn't good, and he went to sleep when he sat down to read the paper.

They recommended Dalmatians because they were especially loyal to their owner, to the person who fed them. That's why they were known as fire department dogs, loyal and fearless in emergencies. They were big dogs, but not too big, and trustworthy around children, and were sometimes called carriage dogs or coach dogs too, because they liked to accompany horses and vehicles and they had style, an air of dignity. Dalmatians were supposed to have come from Dalmatia, which was somewhere in the Balkans.

But Jack did not have dignity. He was the kind of dog that used to be described as crazy-friendly. When Mark tried to train him, the dog's habits seemed to grow worse. "No!" Mark said when Jack jumped up on him with wet paws and licked his chin or his hands. Yesterday he'd ruined Mildred's good suit as she was trying to get into the pickup to go to town.

"Get down, Jack," Mildred had said, but the dog didn't respond, acting like the scolding was praise and even curses were words of endearment. Which they were in a way. How many times had parents said to their children, "This hurts me more than it hurts you"—as they were about to whip them.

"You've really got to do something about that dog," Mildred said again.

Mark loved Jack like the dog was a young child. It surprised him how much he cared about the wayward dog. He didn't remember feeling affection that intense for his children, even when they were little, though maybe that was an illusion of age and the beginning of dementia. But he knew Mildred was right. He either had to train the dog better or get rid of him. And he couldn't bear the thought of calling the dog warden or taking Jack in the pickup to the dog pound where they would put him down.

Since verbal commands seemed to have no effect, Mark tried to think of other ways to discipline the Dalmatian, break his bad habits, really communicate with him. If the dog acted like an unruly child, he would have to be treated like a child, however crazy-friendly he was. All Mark's experience from his own childhood, and as a father, had taught him that children fear a fine switch. A light hickory stings legs without really hurting them. A child will learn respect for a slender hickory. Mark hated the thought of whipping Jack, but finally saw he had no choice. He'd put if off long enough.

Mark was carrying a bucket of water to the little garden beside the house to set out tomato plants when Jack came running from his house. "Stay back!" he said to the Dalmatian, but Jack lunged for his ankles, to press up against him, to show how excited he was to be with his friend and master.

"Now get back," Mark said. He tried to step around the dog, but Jack cut him off. Mark stumbled and fell and the bucket spilled on the grass. As Mark raised to his knees the dog whimpered and licked his face and pushed against his shoulder.

"You dumb mutt!" Mark said, hoping Mildred hadn't seen him fall. When he finally got to his feet, relieved no bones were broken, he walked carefully to the nearest sourwood tree, taking short steps to keep from tripping on Jack, who seemed more excited than ever by the fall and splashed water. Mark broke a sprout from the base of the sourwood, the kind of sprout he used to make arrows when he was a boy. The switch was thinner than a pencil and long as his arm, the size of a witch's wand or the stick a symphony conductor waves. He stripped the leaves off the end, which was springy as the tip of a fly rod.

"Now stand back," Mark said, and threatened with the hickory. But instead of backing away Jack jumped like he thought Mark was playing, teasing him with the stick. He tried to grab the hickory in his teeth and put his paws on Mark's belt.

"You fool," Mark said.

Avoiding the snap of the dog's jaws on the stick, he swung and hit Jack on the shoulder. The pet whimpered and jumped higher to lick his face. Mark swung again and hit the dog across the back. The blow raised the hair in a line along the spine. The dog dropped to the ground and tried to push up against Mark's shins. Instead of backing away, Jack wanted to come closer, to show his affection. The Dalmatian crowded so close he prevented Mark from taking a step. Mark lashed at the dog's shoulder again.

"Got to learn your lesson," he muttered between his teeth. Jack whimpered and pressed closer, following Mark as he stepped back. Mark brought the hickory down on top of the dog's head. He hit Jack on the ears and on his face. He beat him on the nose and Jack yelped but didn't back away. The dog snapped at his hand as though playing a game.

"I'll teach you a lesson, old boy," Mark said with his lips pressed tight. Swinging his arm as hard as he could, he thrashed the dog across the eyes and face. He hit him on the neck and shoulder. He whipped Jack's ears and eyes, and beat the lips and nose again.

Jack yelped and snapped again. "You won't snap at *me*," Mark said. He swung the hickory like he was putting out a fire. He whipped the dog as he'd once whipped hornets with a pine limb as they shot from a nest. But the dog wouldn't back away. Instead of feeling resentment, Jack pushed closer and tried to lick the hand that beat him. He seemed to think that if he could get close enough Mark couldn't reach him, which was partly true, since it was difficult to slash at something pressed against your knees. Mark swung so hard he hit his own leg. I'm so feeble I'm whipping myself, he thought.

The tip of the hickory broke, and the end, held by a tendon of bark, flopped as he wielded the wand. Mark beat harder. He would wear the hickory out and break it in little pieces if he had to, to do his duty. He'd slash the dog until the wand was shreds, if that was what it took to discipline the Dalmatian. He would not give up on the dog, and he would not give it up. He lashed again and again, doing what he had to. He'd owned Jack for over a year, and in that time he'd taught the dog nothing. Mark liked to think that throughout his life he'd met his responsibilities, but now in his old age he confronted failure.

When the switch had broken down to a stub about as long as a pencil, with curls of bark hanging from the end, Mark stopped swinging. He was tired and his wind short. He pitched the remains of the hickory away, and it was only then that he saw the blood on Jack's nose. A trickle of blood oozed from a nostril. He knew the nose was the most sensitive part of a dog's body. There was also blood in one of Jack's eyes.

Tears came to Mark's eyes and a sob tightened his throat. He dropped to his knees and grabbed the dog by the shoulders. "Poor old Jack," he said. "I don't want to hurt you." He hugged the dog as the Dalmatian licked his face. Jack was so excited he lunged forward and pushed Mark off balance so he fell on his side. The dog licked the tears on his cheeks before Mark could roll away and push himself up.

"Looks like you've not taught him much." It was Mildred, who'd brought a plate of scraps from the kitchen for Jack's feeding bowl. Mark refused to answer. He wouldn't argue with Mildred about the training and punishment of Jack, for Jack was *his* dog and none of her business.

When one of their children had done something bad and had to be punished, it was Mark who did it. When Mark, Jr. took a dollar from the church collection plate and was caught by his Sunday School teacher, it was Mark who had to spank him. Mark had hated to confront his son and make him go break a hickory off the sweet shrub bush and bring it to him. It always seemed so awkward to hold the boy by his left hand and whip him across his bottom and legs. It broke a father's heart to have to do it. And Mark hated himself afterward, even though he knew he'd done only what was required of a father. But on sad occasions like that Mildred had always kept in the background. Because he was the man of the house he had to do what was necessary. And now he wouldn't let her tell him how to train his dog.

"Don't tell me what to do," he said to Mildred as she shoved the scraps into Jack's bowl.

"Somebody will have to tell you," Mildred said. "That dog is going to hurt some little kid and then you'll be sued."

"He don't mean no harm," Mark said. But Mildred had already started back to the house with the empty plate.

When they'd gone to get Jack last year and drove up to the house in Dana, he saw the puppies in the pen before even getting out of the truck. Mark walked to the cage to look at the litter of five little Dalmatians, and he spotted Jack first thing. He wasn't the biggest in the litter and he wasn't the littlest, but he was the liveliest. The baby dog leapt up on the cage, put his front paws on the wire, and looked right into Mark's eyes.

Mark couldn't describe how he knew that puppy was his. There was something about the shape, the proportions, and the look on his face. It was hard to say what it was, but from the first Mark felt certain this puppy was the one.

"Pick any one you want," said the owner, a Mr. Morley who worked at the GE plant.

Mildred had selected the biggest puppy, the one that was quiet and calm. She said that one would be the least trouble and the best companion. But it was going to be *his* dog, and Mark said he'd choose the one he wanted, and he pointed out Jack to the owner. Jack and Mark had recognized each other from the start. There was a bond between them from that moment, love at first sight. Mark would never forget the day they brought Jack home, August 16, 1987.

As soon as he ate the scraps in the bowl by the doghouse Jack pricked up his ears. He always listened for the school bus in the afternoon, and it was time for the bus. Jack didn't run after all cars, but he couldn't stay away from the school bus. Mark never knew if that was because the bus was loud and painted bright orange, or because the children yelled at Jack and threw things from the windows. But as soon as the dog heard the bus he dashed out into the road to bark and yelp and jump up on the side and snap at the tires.

"Stay here!" Mark ordered. But Jack was already off and running across the yard and down the bank to the road, barking like he was chasing squirrels. Because it was a warm day, the windows of the bus were open and the children yelled and whistled. Jack ran alongside the bus and yelped and leaped high as he could toward the windows.

"Stop that!" Mark called. But Jack paid no attention. He lunged at the tires and ran along like he was trying to gnaw the door to pieces. Mark hurried toward the road, for he wanted the bus driver to know that he intended to prevent Jack from chasing the bus. The driver might report him to the dog warden and they would fine him or take Jack away.

Mark had had problems with his heart for the past three years, since an episode that put him in the hospital for days and led to bypass surgery. He took three kinds of heart medicine, and he wasn't supposed to get excited or exert himself. But he had to train Jack and break him from running after the bus, if he wanted to keep the dog, if he wanted to have a dog at all. One day Jack was liable to run under the wheels of the bus, or be hit by an oncoming car. Or he might make the bus driver run off the road trying to avoid him. If he didn't teach the dog to behave there were sure to be ugly consequences.

Mark hadn't reached the end of the driveway before his breath grew short and the daylight dimmed. He stepped to an oak tree and held onto the trunk. It seemed like somebody had darkened the sun and twilight had come. He sweated like he'd run a mile, and it seemed all the oxygen had been drawn out of the air. The ground under him heaved like an ocean in a storm and then tilted as though draining away.

Whoa, Mark said to himself and held onto the tree.

"One of these days you'll have another episode and that'll be the end of you," Mildred liked to say. He closed his eyes and heard Jack barking and yipping as he followed the bus. Jack usually ran alongside the bus almost to the church at the corner. For some reason the dog turned back there, like that was the end of his territory. He would come loping back to the house and the bus would go on to deliver the children farther along the river road. Then Jack would come yipping and wagging back into the yard, pretending he'd done nothing wrong.

As Mark's breath returned he saw the hoe handle lying in the weeds by the driveway. It was half an old handle he'd used to punch holes for tomato slips. He let go of the oak tree and picked up the stick just as Jack galloped yipping and whining back into the yard.

"You think you don't have to mind me?" Mark said to the dog. "You think you can do whatever you want?" He saw it was now or never for training the Dalmatian. If he didn't break the dog's bad habits he would lose him. As the dog grew older it would be even harder to teach him. It was already nearly hopeless.

As Jack tried to jump up on him, Mark swung the handle and hit him on the rump. The dog yelped and jumped down and Mark swung again and connected with the head just over the ears. "Stay away from the school bus!" he shouted. Jack tried to push up against Mark's legs as he usually did, whimpering and wagging his tail. Mark whipped him on the rump again, like he was a child, then on the back and hind legs.

Suddenly Mark noticed that Jack didn't walk the way he had before. The dog stepped back, but he hopped, like he was on three legs. The left hind leg was lifted as if he couldn't put weight on it. And it was turned in an odd way, the shape all wrong. Mark had only hit him a few times on the leg. He dropped the hoe handle and reached for Jack.

The dog backed away and Mark grabbed him by the collar. What have I done? he said to himself. He dropped to his knees and looked at the left hind leg. It was certainly broken. There was no doubt of that. The leg might have been broken running after the bus, or the bone cracked by the stick. He didn't know which. "Oh, darling," he said and put his arms around the Dalmatian. Bracing himself carefully he picked the dog up without touching the broken leg. Jack yelped and barked at the air. A dog will snap and cry that way when in pain. Jack panted and drooled and snapped at the empty air. Going slow to avoid stumbling, Mark carried his pet across the yard toward the doghouse.

When Mildred saw him with the dog in his arms she came running from the porch. "What's wrong?" she said.

"I think Jack has broke his leg."

"Then we'll take him to the vet."

"No, I'll fix it myself," Mark said.

"How can you fix it?"

"Look, I will take care of it!" Mark shouted.

He laid Jack down on the picnic table and went to the garage. What he was looking for was a wooden stirring stick, the kind they give you in paint stores. He found one and cut it in two so each half was about five inches long. Then he found some duct tape and a pair of scissors.

Mildred stood by the picnic table to watch and he told her to hold Jack by the collar and not let him move. But the first time he placed the splint on the side of the broken leg the dog jerked and yelped, and the sticks fell to the ground.

"Hold him still, damn it."

"I won't ask how this happened," Mildred said.

As she gripped the collar Mark held the splints on either side of the broken leg, and gently as he could wrapped the tape around the leg and sticks, making the splint as firm as he dared.

"It's going to be hard to pull that tape off," Mildred observed.

"We'll worry about that later," Mark said.

After the splint was in place and Mildred returned to the house, he sat on the bench by the picnic table with his arm around Jack. The dog panted and for once acted resigned, like he was sad but knew he was in loving hands.

•

Mark was proud of the way he'd patched up the broken leg. For the next few days Jack walked on three legs, and then when he walked on four again he limped. When he put too much weight on the hurt leg he yelped and barked, and then whimpered. Mark tried to keep him quiet and still, at least until the leg bones knitted back together.

But it was no use. Jack was too nervous and excitable. Whenever Mark came near him he would run and try to jump up on him. If pushed away, he would rub against Mark's legs, making him stumble. Jack even tried to run after the school bus, though he wasn't as fast as usual. But he could still bark, and he growled and snapped at the bus. It was Mark's responsibility to teach him, and he hadn't taught him a thing. Somewhere he'd read an article about breaking dogs from running cars, but he couldn't recall what it said.

"If you can't teach that dog some manners we'll have to get rid of him," Mildred said for the hundredth time.

"I will not get rid of him."

"Then don't blame me when he causes you or somebody else to break a leg."

Mark was waiting for Jack's leg to heal, and then he was going to have to start working with him in earnest. He would order a book about training Dalmatians. There had to be such a book. He was sure he'd seen one somewhere.

•

It was about a week after Jack broke his leg that a police car drove into the yard and parked beside the pickup. Mark was sitting on the tailgate of the truck sharpening a hoe with a whetrock. Jack came running on three legs from his house, as the deputy got out of the car in his starched uniform, and Jack tried to jump on him. The officer smiled and pushed him away. "Friendly dog," he said and tipped his hat.

"Jack don't mean no harm," Mark said.

"I can see he likes people," the deputy said.

The officer said his name was Alvin Nance and he was from over on Mount Olivet and his folks had known Mark's folks for a hundred years.

"I remember Cephas Nance," Mark said. "He had the mill over on the creek."

"That's the one," the deputy said. Jack crowded up against the creased trousers, and the deputy took a step back. He said he hated to bother anybody, but there had been a complaint about the dog. The school bus driver had stated that Jack ran out in the road and made it dangerous to drive by this house. The driver was afraid he'd wreck the bus trying to avoid the dog. And sometimes Jack followed the bus until it stopped and scared the children as they got off, barking and jumping on them.

"Jack runs alongside the bus," Mark said, "but he turns back before the church."

The deputy said he was sure Jack didn't mean no harm. He could see he was a friendly dog. But the county couldn't afford to have him endangering schoolchildren and scaring them at the bus stop.

"I'm trying to train him," Mark said.

"I know you are, Mr. Evans," Deputy Nance said. He was young enough to be Mark's grandson. In his prime Mark could have picked the deputy up in his pressed uniform and paddled his butt. The young cop took a piece of folded paper out of his shirt pocket and handed it to Mark. "I know you want to do the right thing, Mr. Evans," he said.

Jack tried to jump on the deputy again, but Mark grabbed the dog by the collar. "Quiet, boy," he said.

The deputy tipped his trooper hat and said he hoped Mark would keep the dog secured on his property and not let him run into the road. He got back in the patrol car and started the engine. As he backed away Jack broke loose from Mark and ran alongside the car and barked. He followed the cruiser down the driveway and almost to the church. Mark called after him but it didn't do any good.

The sheet of paper was a citation. Mark got his glasses out and read it, holding the sheet up to the light with trembling hands. The document warned that he must not let his dog harass the school bus or schoolchildren. All dogs must be restrained on their owner's property. If he failed to comply with the directive he could be fined. If he had to be warned twice and didn't correct the problem, the dog could be taken and put down. The paper was dated September 17, 1988.

No cop had ever brought such a warning to Mark's house before. The deputy had embarrassed Mark just when he was trying his best to teach Jack to behave. The cop had taken advantage of his trouble to humiliate him. Mildred stepped out on the porch and called to ask what the deputy had wanted.

"Nothing," Mark said.

"It didn't look like nothing," she said and retreated into the house.

Jack came limping back into the yard, panting from the excitement of running. He rushed up to Mark and tried to jump on his chest, almost knocking Mark over with his weight and enthusiasm.

"I will teach you to jump on people," Mark said. The dog tried to lick his face, and licked his hand that still held the whetrock. Mark saw that he had to teach his dog a lesson now, once and for all, or Jack would never learn anything. There was no choice but to do it, if he wanted to keep Jack. He hit him over the head with the whetstone, but the stone broke in two. It was the kind of whetrock with a wooden handle, the kind you can't get anymore. He'd found the stone in a hardware store in Canton.

Jack whimpered and staggered like he was dazed. The dog whined and licked the hand that held the broken whetstone. That was when the panic rose in Mark, streaming up from his heels and legs and through his belly and chest. The rage seemed to flare out of the ground and through his guts and into his eyes until he could hardly see. What if he could never teach Jack to behave? Was it hopeless? Mark dropped to his knee and beat the dog in the face and eyes with the stub of the whetstone until he was too tired to swing anymore.

When he stopped, Jack lay still on the ground. There was blood on the dog's mouth where several teeth were broken and blood stained the top of his head, caved in like a broken jar. Jack lay on the grass as if he were sleeping.

"Jack," Mark said, "Jack, my dear old buddy."

With a trembling hand he shook the dog's shoulder, but Jack didn't respond. He shook him again. Tossing the bloody whetstone aside he grabbed the Dalmatian's shoulders. There was a gasp of air from the dog's lungs, but he didn't move. The body was warm, but Jack was dead.

"No! Jack," Mark said, and his eyes burned with tears. A sob rose in his throat and the world seemed to grow bleak. He hugged Jack to his chest and heaved so hard he couldn't see. For he didn't know how he could live without his dog, his friend. What would he do with nothing to love, and nothing to love him? Blood smeared on his chin and on his chest as he hugged the body closer. He didn't care if his khaki shirt got ruined. Jack had been his only friend.

Mark's eyes were so blurred with tears he didn't see Mildred approach. She'd watched him from the porch. She put her hands on his shoulders and said everything would be all right.

"It won't be all right; Jack is dead," Mark said.

"I know," Mildred said. "You did what you could to train him."

"His head is crushed."

"You put him down and come into the house," Mildred said. She spoke more kindly than she had in a long time.

"I'll have to bury Jack," Mark said.

"You can do that later," Mildred said. "Now you need to rest." She put her hands under his arms and helped him up. Then with her arm around his waist she led him toward the house. He stumbled, but she kept him steady.

"You'll feel better when you take your pills," Mildred said.

"I won't feel better."

"You'll feel much better." She hugged him tighter.

Mark looked back at Jack lying beside the truck and another sob rose in his throat. The house seemed far away.

About the Author

CHRIS KITCHEN

ROBERT MORGAN is the author of fourteen books of poetry, most recently *Dark Energy* (2015) and *Terroir* (2011). He has also published twelve volumes of fiction, including *Gap Creek* (1999), a *New York Times* bestseller. A sequel, *The Road from Gap Creek*, published in 2013 that received the 2014 Thomas Wolfe Memorial Literary Award, was followed by the novel *Chasing the North Star* (2016) and *As Rain Turns to Snow and Other Stories* (2017). In addition, Morgan is the author of three nonfiction books, *Good Measure: Essays, Interviews, and Notes on Poetry* (1993); *Boone: A Biography* (2007); and *Lions of the West: Heroes and Villains of the Westward Expansion* (2011).

Morgan has been awarded the James G. Hanes Poetry Prize by the Fellowship of Southern Writers and the Academy Award in Literature by the American Academy of Arts and Letters, and is the recipient of fellowships from the Guggenheim Foundation, the Rockefeller Foundation, the National Endowment for the Arts, and the New York State Arts Council. In 2013 he received the History Award Medal from the Daughters of the American Revolution. His first play, *Homemade Yankees*, was awarded the East Tennessee Civil War Alliance John Cullum Drama Prize. He has served as visiting writer at Davidson College and at Furman, Duke, Appalachian State, and East Carolina universities. A member of the Fellowship of Southern Writers, he was inducted into the North Carolina Literary Hall of Fame in 2010.

Morgan was born in Hendersonville, North Carolina in 1944. He taught from 1971 to 2022 at Cornell University, where he was Kappa Alpha Professor of English.